The Golden
Book

Birthday

By
MARGARET WISE BROWN

Illustrated by
LEONARD WEISGARD

A GOLDEN BOOK • NEW YORK
Western Publishing Company, Inc.,
Racine, Wisconsin 53404

One spring,
deep in the woods,
these animals
were born:

a worm,

a bee,

a squirrel,

a wild pig,

and, of course,
    a little rabbit.

The next spring they all had a birthday because they were one year old. Each animal got a birthday present. A present, of course, is something you want.

Here comes a little worm,
squirming, squirming, squirm.
Happy birthday, little worm.
You'll get your present soon—
BOOM!

A worm was having a birthday.

"Happy birthday, Worm," said his mother. She gave him an apple.

"Squish," said the little worm. He squished his thanks.

Here comes a little bee,
  a buzzing busy bee.
    Happy birthday, little bee.
      You'll get your present soon—
        BOOM!

A bee was having a birthday.
All the bees were
    flying around him
        with presents of pollen.
But his mother
    had the biggest present.
She was flying with it
    from a long way off.

BzzzzzzzzzzzzzzzzzzzzzZZZZZZ

BzzzzzzzzzzzzzzzzzzzzzzzZZZZZ

The little bee reached forth his five feet to take
it while he stood on his sixth foot.
　　It was a

　　　SNAPDRAGON!

　　The little bee buried his face in it
　　　and buzzed
　　　　　his thanks.

Here comes a little squirrel,
his tail a-twitch and a-whirl.
Happy birthday, little squirrel.
You'll get your present soon—
BOOM!

A squirrel was having a birthday.

What would a squirrel like for his birthday?
A squirrel would like a nut. And that is just what
he got, three of them.

"Crack a nut," said his mother.

"Crack a nut," said his father.

"Crack a nut," said his sister.

The little squirrel chattered his thanks.

Here comes a little wild pig,
jiggety, jiggety, jig.
Happy birthday, little pig.
You'll get your present soon—
BOOM!

A pig was having a birthday—a little wild pig.

"Happy birthday, dear Pig," said Mother Pig. "Here is a birthday present."

A birthday present for a pig, of course, is something a pig would like. What do you think it was?

The little pig grunted,
  "Oink, oink, oink."
They brought him to a swamp
  of sun-warmed dirt to roll in!
The little wild pig squealed his delight
  and his thanks.

Here comes a little rabbit.
If he sees a carrot he'll grab it.
Happy birthday, little rabbit.
You'll get your present soon—
BOOM!

A little rabbit was having a birthday.
With a hop, skip, and a jump he arose
in the morning.
And his own true rabbit gave him a lovely
bright crisp carrot.

The little rabbit nibbled his thanks.

Then all the animals sang a song.

"Thanks for the apple and the nuts,
　　thanks for the snapdragon,
　　　　thanks for the big carrot,
　　　　　　and thanks for the swamp and the sun."

"And thank you again for the carrot," said
the little rabbit before anyone could grab it away
from him.